W9-AKL-472

CUBA LIBRE

Elmore Leonard

CUBA LIBRE

WHEELER PUBLISHING, INC.
ROCKLAND, MA
★ AN AMERICAN COMPANY ★

Published in Large Print by arrangement with Delacorte Press, a division of Bantam Doubleday Dell Publishing Group, Inc. in the United States and Canada.

Wheeler Large Print Book Series.

Set in 16 pt Plantin.

Library of Congress Cataloging-in-Publication Data

Elmore, Leonard, 1925
Cuba Libre / by Elmore Leonard.
p. (large print) cm.(Wheeler large print book series)
ISBN 1-56895-600-2 (hardcover)
1. Cuba—History—Revolution, 1895–1898—Fiction. 2. Spanish-American War, 1898—Fiction. 3. Americans—Travel—Cuba—Fiction. 4. Historical fiction. gsafd. 5. Adventure stories. gsafd. 6. Large type books.
I. Title. II. Series
[PS3562.E55C83 1998b]
813′.54—dc21

98-026431
CIP

For my old friend Allan Hayes

ONE

Tyler arrived with the horses February eighteenth, three days after the battleship *Maine* blew up in Havana harbor. He saw buzzards floating in the sky the way they do but couldn't make out what they were after. This was off Morro Castle, the cattle boat streaming black smoke as it came through the narrows.

But then pretty soon he saw a ship's mast and a tangle of metal sticking out of the water, gulls resting on it. One of the Mexican deckhands called to the pilot tug bringing them in, wanting to know what the wreckage was. The pilot yelled back it was the *Maine.*

Yeah? The main what? Tyler's border Spanish failed to serve, trying to make out voices raised against the wind. The deckhand told him it was a *buque de guerra,* a warship.

Earlier that month he had left Sweetmary in the Arizona Territory by rail: loaded thirty-one mares aboard Southern Pacific stock cars and rode them all the way to Galveston on the Gulf of Mexico. Here he was met by his partner in this deal, Charlie Burke, Tyler's foreman at one time, years ago. Charlie Burke introduced him to a little Cuban mulatto—"Ben Tyler, Victor Fuentes"—the man appearing to be a good sixty years old, though it was hard to tell, his skin the color of mahogany.

Fuentes inspected the mares, none more than six years old or bigger than fifteen hands, checked each one's conformation and teeth, Fuentes wiping his hands on the pants of his white suit, picked twenty-five out of the bunch, all bays, browns and sorrels, and said he was sure they could sell the rest for the same money, one hundred fifty dollars each. He said Mr. Boudreaux was going to like these girls and would give them a check for thirty-seven hundred fifty dollars drawn on the Banco de Comercio before they left Havana. Fuentes said he would expect only five hundred of it for his services.

Tyler said to Charlie Burke, later, the deal sounded different than the way he'd originally explained it.

Charlie Burke said the way you did business in Cuba was the same as it worked in Mexico, everybody getting their cut. Tyler said, what he meant, he thought they were going directly from here to Matanzas, where Boudreaux's sugar estate was located. Charlie Burke said he thought so too; but Boudreaux happened to be in Havana this week and next. It meant they'd take the string off the boat, put the horses in stock pens for the man to look at, reload them and go on to Matanzas. What Tyler wanted to know, and Charlie Burke didn't have the answer: "Who pays for stopping in Havana?"

That evening Charlie Burke and Mr. Fuentes left on a Ward Line steamer bound for Havana.

It was late the next day Tyler watched his mares brought aboard the cattle boat, the name *Vamoose* barely readable on its rusted hull. Next came bales of hay and some oats, one of the stock handlers saying you didn't want a horse to eat much out at sea. Tyler stepped aboard with his saddle and gear to mind the animals himself. That was fine with the stock handlers; they had the cattle to tend. They said the trip would take five days.

It was back toward the end of December Charlie Burke had wired: FOUND WAY TO GET RICH WITH HORSES.

He came out on the train from East Texas and was waiting for Tyler the first day of the new year, 1898, on the porch of the Congress Hotel in Sweetmary, a town named for a copper mine, LaSalle Street empty going on 10:00 A.M., the mine shut down and the town sleeping off last night.

Charlie Burke came out of the rocking chair to watch Tyler walking his dun mare this way past the Gold Dollar, past I.S. Weiss Mercantile, past the Maricopa Bank—Charlie Burke watching him looking hard at the bank as he came along. Tyler brought the dun up to the porch railing and said, "You know what horses are going for in Kansas City?"

"Tell me," Charlie Burke said.

"Twenty-five cents a head."

They hadn't seen each other in almost four years.

Charlie Burke said, "Then we don't want to go to Kansas City, do we?"

He watched Tyler chew on that as he stepped down from the dun and came up on the porch. They took time now to hug each other, Charlie Burke's mind going back to the boy who'd come out here dying to work for a cattle outfit and ride horses for pay. Ben Tyler, sixteen years old and done with school, St. Simeon something or other for Boys, in New Orleans, this one quicker than the farm kids who wandered out from Missouri and Tennessee. Charlie Burke, foreman of the Circle-Eye at the time, as many as thirty riders under him spring through fall, put the boy to work chasing mustangs and company stock that had quit the bunch, and watched this kid gentle the green ones with a patience you didn't find in most hands. Watched him trail-boss herds they brought down in Old Mexico and drove to graze. Watched him quit the big spread after seven years to work for a mustanger named Dana Moon, supplying horses to mine companies and stage lines and remounts to the U.S. cavalry. Watched him take over the business after Moon was made Indian agent at White Tanks, a Mimbreño Apache subagency north of town. The next thing he saw of Ben Tyler was his face on a wanted poster above the notice:

$500 REWARD
DEAD OR ALIVE

What happened, Tyler's business fell on hard times and he took to robbing banks. So then the next time Charlie Burke actually saw him was out in the far reaches of the territory at Yuma Prison: convicts and their visitors sitting across from one another at tables placed end to end down the center of the mess hall. Mothers, wives, sweethearts all wondering how their loved ones would fare in this stone prison known as the Hell Hole on the Bluff; Charlie Burke wondering why, if Tyler had made up his mind to rob banks, he chose the Maricopa branch in Sweetmary, where he was known.

He said on account of it was the closest one.

Charlie Burke said, "I come all the way out here to watch you stare past me at the wall?"

So then Tyler said, all right, because it was where LaSalle Mining did their banking and LaSalle Mining owed him nine hundred dollars. "Four times I went up the hill to collect," Tyler said in his prison stripes and haircut, looking hard and half starved. "Try and find anybody in charge can cut a check. I went to the Maricopa Bank, showed the teller a .44 and withdrew the nine hundred from the mine company's account."

"That's how you do business, huh?"

"Hatch and Hodges owed me twelve hundred the day they shut down their line. They said don't worry, you'll get your money. I waited another four months, the same as I did with LaSalle, and drew it out of their bank over in Benson."

"Who else owed you money?"

"Nobody."

"But you robbed another bank."

"Yeah, well, once we had the hang of it...I'm kidding. It wasn't like Red and I got drunk and went out and robbed a bank. Red worked for Dana Moon before he came with me, had all that experience, so I offered him a share, but he'd only work for wages. After we did the two banks I paid Red what he had coming and he bought a suit of clothes cost him ten dollars, and wanted to put the rest in the bank. We're in St. David at the time. We go to the bank to open a savings account and the bank refused him. I asked the manager, was it on account of Red being Warm Springs Apache? The manager become snotty and one thing led to another...."

"You robbed the bank to teach him manners."

"Red was about to shoot him."

"Speaking of shooting people," Charlie Burke said, prompting his friend the convict.

"We were on the dodge by then," Tyler said, "wanted posters out on us. To some people that five hundred reward looked like a year's wages. These fellas I *know* were horse thieves—they ran my stock more than once—they got after us for the reward, followed our tracks all the way to Nogales and threw down on us in a cantina—smoky place, had a real low ceiling."

"The story going around," Charlie Burke said, "they pulled, Ben Tyler pulled and shot all three of them dead."

"Maybe, though I doubt it. All the guns going off in there and the smoke, it was hard to tell. We came back across the border, the deputies were waiting there to run us down."

"Have you learned anything?"

"Always have fresh horses with you."

"You've become a smart aleck, huh?"

"Not around here. They put you in leg irons."

"What do you need I can get you?"

"Some books, magazines. Dana Moon sends me the Chicago *Times* he gets from some fella he knows."

"You don't seem to be doing too bad."

"Considering I live in a cell with five hot-headed morons and bust rocks into gravel all day. I've started teaching Mr. Rinning's children how to ride the horsey and they like me. Mr. Rinning's the superintendent; he says to me, 'You're no outlaw, you're just stupid—a big educated fella like you robbing banks?' He says if I'm done being stupid I'll be out as soon as I do three years."

Charlie Burke said to him that day in the Yuma mess hall, "Are you done?"

"I was mad is all, those people owing me money I'd worked hard for. Yeah, I got it out of my system," Tyler said. "But you know what? There ain't nothing to robbing a bank."

He was back at the Circle-Eye riding the winter range, looking for late calves or ones that had dodged the roundup.

Giving each other that hug, Charlie Burke felt the shape of a revolver beneath Tyler's sheepskin hanging open. Stepping back, he pulled the coat open a little more, enough to see the .44 revolver hanging in a shoulder rig.

"You have somebody mad at you?" Charlie Burke speaking, as usual, through his big mustache and a wad of Mail Pouch.

"You don't ever want to win fame as an outlaw," Tyler said, "unless everybody knows you've done your time. There're people who save wanted dodgers and keep an eye out. They see me riding up the street and think, Why, there's five hundred dollars going by. Next thing I know, I'm trying to explain the situation to these men holding Winchesters on me. I've been shot at twice out on the graze, long range. Another time I'm in a line shack, a fella rode right into my camp and pulled on me."

"You shot him?"

"I had to. Now I got his relatives looking for me. It's the kind of thing never ends."

"Well," Charlie Burke said, "you should never've robbed those banks."

Tyler said, "Thanks for telling me."

They sat in rocking chairs on the shaded hotel porch, the day warming up, Charlie Burke in town clothes, a dark suit and necktie, his hat off now to show his pure white forehead, thin hair plastered across his scalp. In no hurry. He said, "If the market ain't Kansas City, where you suppose it is?"

"I'm trying to think," Tyler said, sounding tired from a life of scratching by and those years busting rocks, his long legs stretched out, run-down boots resting on the porch rail. A saddle tramp, if Charlie Burke didn't know better. The boy had weathered to appear older than his thirty or so years, his light tan J. B. Stetson favoring one eye as he turned his head to look at Charlie Burke, the hat stained and shaped forever with a gentle curl to the brim.

"You've been reading about the gold fields," Tyler said. "Take a string up to Skagway, not a soul around last year, now there're three thousand miners, a dozen saloons and a couple whorehouses on the site. I suppose put the horses on a boat, it's too far to trail drive. I've thought about it myself," Tyler said, though he didn't sound fond of the idea.

That pleased Charlie Burke, his plans already laid. He said, "You could do that. But if you're gonna take a boat ride, where'd you rather go, to a town where people live in tents stiff with the cold, or one that's been there since Columbus, four hundred years?" He saw Tyler smile; he knew. "Has palm trees and pretty little dark-eyed girls and you don't freeze to death you step outside."

"So we're talking about Cuba," Tyler said, "and you thought of me because I've been there."

"I thought of you 'cause horses do what you tell 'em. I recall though," Charlie Burke said, still in no hurry, "your daddy ran a sugar mill down there, when you were a kid."

"The mill," Tyler said, "what they call a sugar plantation. The mill itself they call the *central*. Yeah, I was nine years old the summer we went to visit."

"I thought you lived there a while."

"One summer's all. My dad wanted us with him, but my mother said she'd lay across the railroad tracks if he didn't book us passage home. My mother generally had her way. She was afraid if we stayed through the rainy season we'd all die of yellow fever. Seven years later her and both my sisters died of influenza. And my dad, he came back to New Orleans to run a sugarhouse out in the parish, the old Belle Alliance, and was killed in an accident out there."

Charlie Burke took time to suck on his chewing tobacco, raise up the chair and spit a stream of juice at the hard-packed street.

"You recall much of Cuba?"

"I remember it being green and humid, nothing like this hardscrabble land. Cuba, you can always find shade when you want some. The only thing ugly are the sugar mills, black smoke pouring out the chimneys...."

"You have a feeling for that place, don't you?"

"Sixteen years old, I was either going back to Cuba or come out here, and hopping a freight was cheaper than taking a boat."

"Well, this trip won't cost you a cent, and you'll make a pile of money before you're through."

Tyler said, "What about the war going on down there? It was in the paper the whole time I was at Yuma, the Cubans fighting for their independence."

They were getting to it now.

"It isn't anything like a real war," Charlie